For Sheck

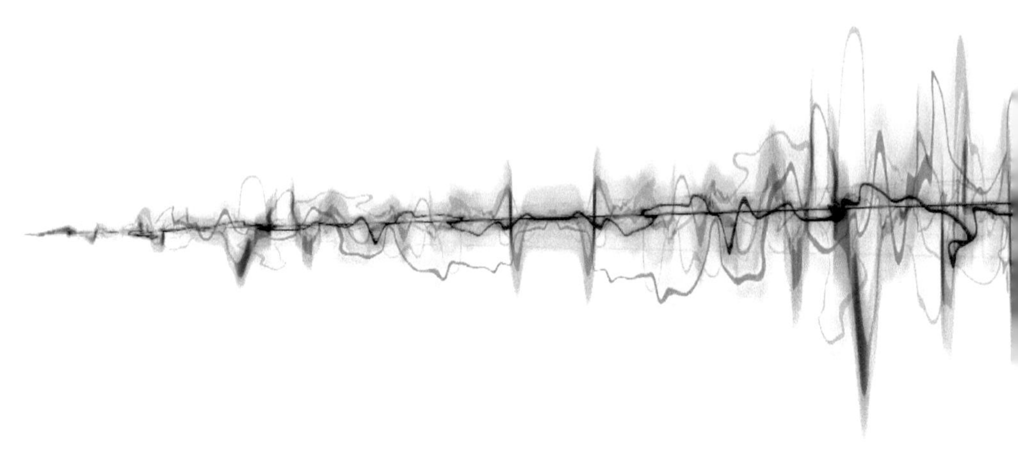

Broken

a play by

C. E. Gatchalian

New Bard Press

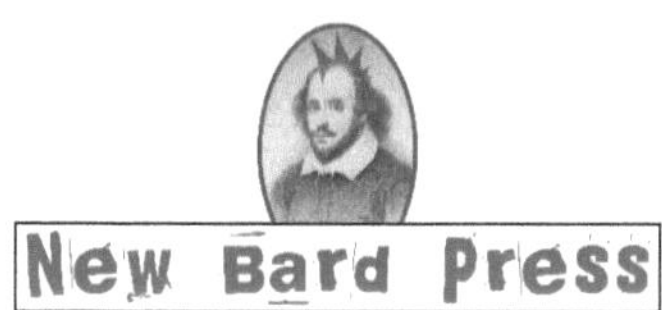

Broken first published in 2006 by
New Bard Press
3238 - 23rd Street, Edmonton, Canada, T6T 2A9
email: newbardpress@shaw.ca
website: http://www.lulu.com/newbardpress

Unless otherwise stated, all photographs by Michael O'Shea.
Used with permission.

This play is a work of fiction. Names, characters, places, and incidents either are the product of the author's imagination or are used fictitiously.

Gatchalian, C. E., 1974-
Broken
A play
ISBN 978-1-84728-866-0

Playwright's Notes:

Broken began its life as an ad hoc collection of five short plays, some previously published by The New Hogarth Press and The Writers' Collective. Initially, it had been an issue of pragmatism – what do you do if you want to stage a series of shorts? You bill them together, of course. Something happened, however, as I reread the plays with my director, Sean Cummings. The plays began to fuse into a single narrative, revealing themselves to us in new and unexpected ways. As rehearsals drew near, it became clear that we had a single full-length play on our hands. We decided to call it *Broken*.

The bones of the original five shorts are still visible beneath the new work's flesh. Those familiar with my work will recognize that *Ticks*, *Motifs & Repetitions*, *Diamond*, *Star*, and *Hands* are still much as they once were, save for a few line and blocking changes and some new names. Thanks to *Broken*, I trust they will also now see these pieces in a brand new light.

C.E. Gatchalian
Vancouver, 2006

Acknowledgments:

Special thanks to Sean Cummings for pulling it all together; to Rob Bartel of New Bard Press for superb and insightful dramaturgy; and to Amanda Lockitch, Brian McGugan and Bryan Wade for their invaluable feedback.

Production History:

Broken premiered at Vancouver's Firehall Arts Centre, March 2nd, 2006, where it was produced by **Meta.for Theatre Company** and **Broken Whisper** with the following cast:

MARY	Tanja Dixon-Warren*
PHILIP	Michael Fera
CATHY	Ntsikie Kheswa
ADRIAN	Thrasso Petras
JEFF	Nelson Wong

-=-

DIRECTOR	Sean Cummings
ASSISTANT DIRECTOR	Jeffrey Fisher
STAGE MANAGER	Niki Boyd
SET DESIGNER	Yvan Morissette
LIGHTING DESIGNER	Mélissa C. Powell
COSTUME DESIGNER	Moira Fentum
SOUND DESIGNER	Sean Cummings
DRAMATURGE	Amanda Lockitch

This production was made possible by the generous support of the **Firehall Arts Centre**, the **City of Vancouver**, and the **BC Arts Council**.

---

* Tanja Dixon-Warren was nominated for the 2006 Jessie Richardson Award, Outstanding Performance by an Actress in a Leading Role.

Set Design:

For the 2006 Firehall production, Yvan Morissette designed an abstract and minimalist set of five rectangular frames, each painted white and placed askew. The first was placed atop a black riser for use as both a table and a bench. The second and third were suspended from the ceiling, hung vertically to enclose the left and right scrims referred to in “Ticks.” The fourth and fifth frames were also suspended from the ceiling but were positioned horizontally above the centre riser.

Yvan Morissette’s minimalist set adorns the stage.

Scene 1

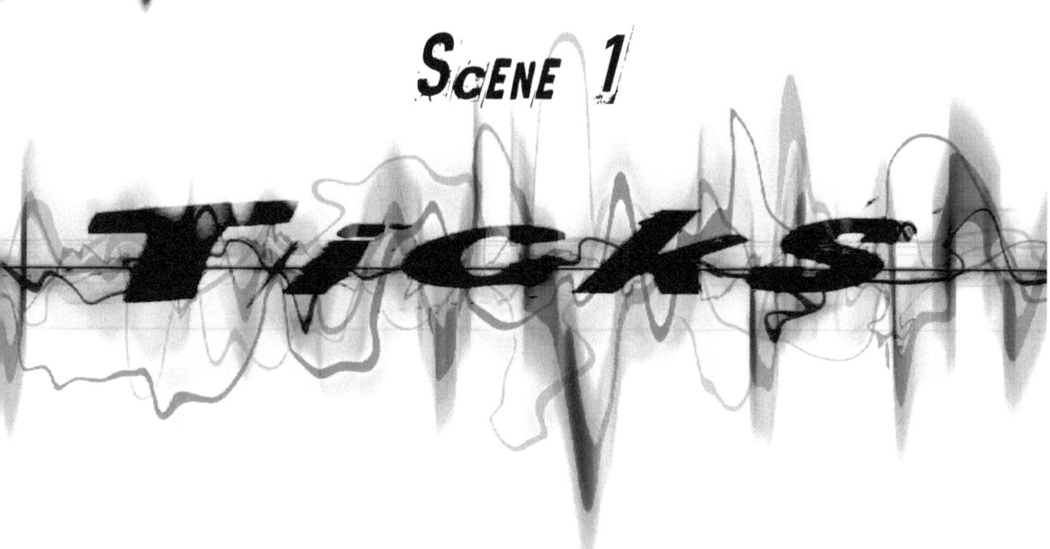

(It's dark. Sounds of traffic and city life mingle with nightclub jazz. Lights up on **Adrian,** *naked, with his back to the audience. He puts on underwear, pants, shirt, shoes. A metronome rests on the table, set to 40 but not yet released.* **Adrian** *picks up the metronome and releases the pendulum rod. He lets it tick seven times before beginning to speak. Each accent symbol in the following speech coincides with a tick of the metronome. The end of each line coincides with another.)*

Adrian: Ýou. *(Tick.)*
Are their háilstorm. *(Tick.)*
Their éarthquake. *(Tick.)*
Their líght. *(Tick.)*
The bówl you hóld in your hánds. *(Tick.)*
The ánswer. *(Tick.)*
Is ýours. *(Tick.)*
Óne. *(Tick.)*
Twó. *(Tick.)*
Thrée. *(Tick.)*

Fóur. *(Tick.)*
Fíve. *(Tick.)*
Síx. *(Tick.)*
Séven. *(Tick.)*
Óne. *(Tick.)*
Mále. *(Tick.)*

*(**Man 1** appears behind left scrim.)*

Mídnight. *(Tick.)*
Párk. *(Tick.)*
Wínk. Nód. Jóin. *(Tick.)*
Twó. *(Tick.)*
Fémale. *(Tick.)*

*(**Woman 1** appears behind right scrim.)*

Mídnight. *(Tick.)*
Bár. *(Tick.)*
Wínk. Nód. Jóin. *(Tick.)*
Thrée. *(Tick.)*
Mále. *(Tick.)*

*(**Man 2** appears behind left scrim.)*

Mídnight. *(Tick.)*
Bánk. *(Tick.)*
Wínk. Nód. Jóin. *(Tick.)*
Fóur. *(Tick.)*

*(**Woman 2** appears behind right scrim.)*

Fémale. *(Tick.)*
Mídnight. *(Tick.)*
Stóre. *(Tick.)*

Wínk. Nód. Jóin. *(Tick.)*
Fíve. *(Tick.)*
Mále. *(Tick.)*

*(**Man 3** appears behind left scrim.)*

Mídnight. *(Tick.)*
Púmp. *(Tick.)*
Wínk. Nód. Jóin. *(Tick.)*
Síx. *(Tick.)*
Fémale. *(Tick.)*

*(**Woman 3** appears behind right scrim.)*

Mídnight. *(Tick.)*
Cáfe. *(Tick.)*
Wínk. Nód. Jóin. *(Tick.)*
Séven. *(Tick.)*
Mále. *(Tick.)*

*(**Man 4** appears behind left scrim.)*

Mídnight. *(Tick.)*
Chúrch. *(Tick.)*
Wínk. Nód. Jóin. *(Tick.)*
Nét. *(Tick.)*
Of líght. *(Tick.)*
The cíty *(Tick.)*
you físh *(Tick.)*
from the dárk. *(Tick.)*
Lámp. *(Tick.)*
Unto féet. *(Tick.)*
Líght. *(Tick.)*
Unto páth. *(Tick.)*
The bówl *(Tick.)*

you hóld *(Tick.)*
in your hánds. *(Tick.)*
The ánswer. *(Tick.)*
Is yóurs. *(Tick.)*

*Ntsikie Kheswa as **Woman 3**, Thrasso Petras as **Adrian**, and Nelson Wong as **Man 4** in "Ticks."*

Scene 2

*(The metronome continues to tick. **Cathy** and **Jeff** enter pools of light to the left and right of **Adrian**. All face the audience.)*

Adrian: Jeff.

Jeff: Cathy.

Cathy: Adrian.

(Pause.)

Adrian: Say it.

Jeff: Somebody.

Cathy: Say it.

(Pause.)

Adrian?

ADRIAN: Cathy?

CATHY: He's OK.

ADRIAN: She's OK.

CATHY He's a bit shy.

ADRIAN: She's a bit shy.

CATHY: But he's OK.

ADRIAN: She's OK.

CATHY: It's nothing serious.

ADRIAN: It's nothing serious.

CATHY: I mean we haven't *done* anything.

ADRIAN: I'm not sure she wants me to.

CATHY: Not that I want him to.

ADRIAN: I'm not sure *I* want to.

CATHY: It's not that I love him.

ADRIAN: I can't say I love her.

CATHY: But by now he should've at least *tried* something.

(ADRIAN stops the metronome.)

ADRIAN: I don't love anyone.

(ADRIAN gives the metronome to JEFF who exits with it.)

CATHY: Adrian.

ADRIAN: *(Turns to CATHY.)* Cathy.

CATHY: *(Walks to platform.)* Well.

ADRIAN: Well.

CATHY: *(Sits.)* Nice night.

ADRIAN: What?

CATHY: Nice night.

ADRIAN: It's OK. *(Pause.)* About tonight.

CATHY: That's OK.

ADRIAN: *(Crosses to CATHY.)* I'm sorry.

CATHY: Don't worry about it.

ADRIAN: I'm just really old-fashioned.

CATHY: I understand.

(ADRIAN sits. Pause.)

ADRIAN: I like your socks.

CATHY: What?

ADRIAN: *(Pushes up* CATHY*'s legs with his.)* Your socks.

CATHY: My socks.

ADRIAN: Yeah.

CATHY: You should.

ADRIAN: Yeah?

CATHY: They're from Germany.

ADRIAN: Oh.

CATHY: Straight from Germany.

ADRIAN: Oh.

(Pause.)

CATHY: Did you like my teacups?

ADRIAN: Your what?

CATHY: Teacups.

ADRIAN: Teacups?

CATHY: Yeah.

ADRIAN: Loved them.

CATHY: Really?

ADRIAN: Truly.

CATHY: Did you like the designs?

ADRIAN: The designs?

CATHY: On the teacups.

ADRIAN: The teacups.

CATHY: Blue and pink flowers with butterflies flying around them.

ADRIAN: Oh, *that.*

CATHY: Yeah, that.

ADRIAN: Yeah.

CATHY: Yeah.

(They both look away. Pause.)

ADRIAN: I like your socks.

CATHY: Thanks.

(Pause.)

ADRIAN Listen.

CATHY: Yeah?

(Pause.)

Adrian & Cathy: *(Together, facing each other.)* I wanna call it off. *(They laugh awkwardly. Pause. Together again.)* I'm just not ready. *(They laugh awkwardly. Pause.)*

Adrian: About tonight.

Cathy: That's OK.

Adrian: I'm sorry.

Cathy: Don't worry about it.

Adrian: I'm just really old-fashioned.

Cathy: I understand.

(Pause.)

Adrian: I like your socks.

Cathy: Thanks.

Adrian: *(Kisses* **Cathy***'s cheek.)* Bye. *(Exits.)*

Cathy: Bye.

(Pool of light on **Cathy***, stage right. Pool of light on* **Jeff***, stage left. They face the audience.)*

Jeff: Cathy?

Cathy: Jeff?

JEFF: What can I say?

CATHY: He's gorgeous.

JEFF: Her hair.

CATHY: His face.

JEFF: *(Getting excited.)* Her breasts.

CATHY: *(Getting excited.)* His chest.

JEFF: Her legs.

CATHY: His butt.

JEFF: And up.

CATHY: And down.

JEFF: *(Comes.)* Oh, God.

CATHY: *(Comes.)* Jesus fuck!

JEFF: What can I say?

(JEFF and CATHY turn to each other.)

CATHY: Nothing much.

JEFF: What's there to say?

CATHY: Nothing much.

(They walk towards each other, arms outstretched.)

JEFF: We don't talk much.

CATHY: It would ruin everything.

(They join hands, move in a circle.)

JEFF: We're just fucking machines.

CATHY: We're nothing to each other.

JEFF: It's better that way.

CATHY: And I want it that way.

*(**JEFF** pulls **CATHY** in, holds her from behind.)*

CATHY: Baby.

JEFF: Baby.

CATHY: I've waited all day for this.

JEFF: So have I.

CATHY: God you're gorgeous.

JEFF: So are you.

CATHY: Your face.

JEFF: Your hair.

Cathy: Your chest.

Jeff: Your breasts.

Cathy: Your butt.

Jeff: Your legs.

Cathy: Your—

Jeff: Cathy?

Cathy: What?

Jeff: Shut the fuck up.

Cathy: *(Turns to face* ***Jeff****.)* Huh?

Jeff: Your mouth should be doing something else.

Cathy: Right.

(She kneels down and unzips his pants. A knock on the door.)

Jeff: Shit.

Cathy: I'll just be a minute.

Jeff: Hurry up.

Cathy: I will.

(CATHY answers door, JEFF sits on the platform.)

Adrian.

ADRIAN: Cathy.

CATHY: What do you want?

ADRIAN: I just—

CATHY: Yeah?

ADRIAN: Well, I—

CATHY: Yeah?

ADRIAN: *(Noticing JEFF.)* Who's that?

CATHY: Who?

ADRIAN: Jeff?

JEFF: Yo.

ADRIAN: Jeff?

JEFF: Ade.

CATHY: *(Crosses to stage left.)* You know each other?

JEFF & ADRIAN: *(Together.)* We're best friends.

CATHY: Jesus fuck.

ADRIAN: *(To JEFF.)* Your fly's open.

JEFF: I know.

ADRIAN: Oh, my God!

CATHY: Jesus fuck.

JEFF: *(To ADRIAN.)* What are you doing here?

ADRIAN: *(Upset, crossing to JEFF.)* I'll never forgive you!

JEFF: Calm down.

ADRIAN: *(Pushes on JEFF's chest; JEFF falls back.)* I'll never forgive you!

CATHY: *(To ADRIAN.)* Wait.

ADRIAN: What?

CATHY: Jeff.

JEFF: Yo.

CATHY: Could you leave us alone?

JEFF: You and Ade?

CATHY: Please.

JEFF: Hurry up.

CATHY: I will.

JEFF: See you, Ade.

(JEFF exits.)

ADRIAN: Wow.

CATHY: What?

ADRIAN: You heal fast.

CATHY: What?

ADRIAN: Nothing.

CATHY: *(Crosses to stage right.)* What?

ADRIAN: Forget it.

CATHY: Wait.

ADRIAN: What?

CATHY: Why did you come?

ADRIAN: No reason.

CATHY: Bullshit.

ADRIAN: No reason.

CATHY: Bullshit!

(Silence. CATHY crosses to stage left.)

Adrian: Cathy.

*(**Cathy** turns to **Adrian**.)*

Cathy: Yeah?

(Pause.)

Adrian: Nothing.

(Pause.)

Cathy: Yeah. *(Pause.)* Adrian.

(Pause.)

Adrian: Yeah?

(Pause.)

Cathy: Nothing.

(Pause.)

Adrian: Yeah.

*(**Adrian** exits. **Jeff** enters.)*

Jeff: Cathy.

Cathy: Jeff.

Jeff: You know him?

Cathy: Who?

JEFF: Ade?

CATHY: Oh.

JEFF: Yeah.

CATHY: We dated.

JEFF: Uh-huh. *(Sits on platform.)*

CATHY: It was nothing.

JEFF: Uh-huh.

CATHY: It was nothing!

(Pause.)

JEFF: Are you all right?

CATHY: I will be.

JEFF: Yeah?

CATHY: If you fuck me.

(Beat of darkness. Pools of light on ***JEFF*** *and* ***CATHY****. They are facing the audience.)*

JEFF: Fuck.

CATHY: Fuck.

JEFF: That's all we ever do.

CATHY: And that's all I want.

JEFF: That's all I ever promised her.

CATHY: And that's all I ever wanted.

JEFF: I'm seeing other girls.

CATHY: Who cares if he does?

JEFF: So what? I don't love her.

CATHY: He's nothing to me.

JEFF: We're just fucking machines.

CATHY: We're nothing to each other.

JEFF: I don't believe in love.

CATHY: There's no such thing.

JEFF: I don't love anyone.

CATHY: And I never will.

*(Beat of darkness. Light on **JEFF** and **CATHY** in the middle of a vicious fight.)*

JEFF: Why the fuck are you so upset?

CATHY: I'm not talking to you!

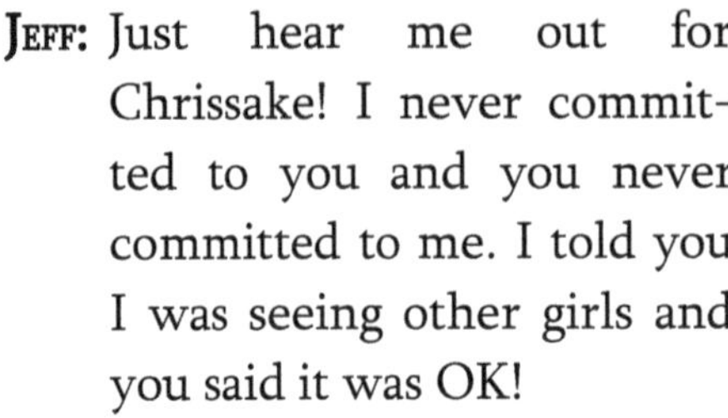

JEFF: Just hear me out for Chrissake! I never committed to you and you never committed to me. I told you I was seeing other girls and you said it was OK!	**CATHY:** *(Singing, hands over ears.)* "My bonny lies over the ocean, my bonny lies over the sea, my bonny lies over the ocean, oh, bring back my bonny to me."

CATHY: Go ahead. Fuck those floosies.

JEFF: Cathy.

CATHY: But not while I'm looking!

JEFF: *(Grabbing her.)* Cathy!

CATHY: *(Tries to pull away.)* Let go!

JEFF: You're a fucking turn-off, you know that?

*(**CATHY** spits in his face. **JEFF** crushes her hand.)*

JEFF: *(Still holding her hand.)* I'm sorry… I'm sorry… I'm sorry…	**CATHY:** Let go of me, you bastard! Let go of me!

*(**CATHY** starts to cry. Pause. They look at each other. Silence.)*

JEFF: Cathy.

(Pause.)

CATHY: Yeah?

(Pause.)

JEFF: Nothing.

(Pause.)

CATHY: Yeah. *(JEFF crosses to stage right.)* Jeff.

(JEFF stops.)

JEFF: Yeah?

(Pause.)

CATHY: Nothing.

(Pause.)

JEFF: Yeah.

(ADRIAN enters. Pools of light on ADRIAN, stage right; JEFF, centre; CATHY, stage left. All face the audience.)

ADRIAN: I can't think straight.

JEFF: I can't work.

CATHY: I can't sleep.

ADRIAN: I can't eat.

CATHY: All I do is eat.

ADRIAN: I feel sick.

CATHY: All I do is puke.

ADRIAN: I can't think straight.

JEFF: This throbbing headache.

CATHY: All I think is Jeff.

JEFF: All I think is Cathy.

CATHY: All I think is Adrian.

JEFF: Cathy.

ADRIAN: Jeff.

CATHY: Adrian.

ADRIAN: Cathy.

JEFF: This throbbing headache.

ADRIAN: This thing burning inside me.

CATHY: It's like a fever.

ADRIAN: It's burning me up.

JEFF: It's making me sick.

CATHY: It's making me puke.

ADRIAN: Who asked you?

Jeff: Who asked you?

Cathy: Who the fuck asked you?

Adrian: Swallow it.

Jeff: Swallow it.

Cathy: Swallow your fucking pride.

Jeff: I need you.

Adrian: I need you.

Cathy: Both of you.

Adrian: Both of you.

Cathy: Jeff.

Jeff: Cathy.

Cathy: Adrian.

Adrian: Help me!

*(**Cathy** exits. **Adrian** steps on platform.)*

Jeff: Adrian?

Adrian: Jeff?

Jeff: Ade's a nice guy.

Adrian: Jeff.

Jeff: We've known each other since first grade.

Adrian: Jeff.

Jeff: He was a bit of a sissy.

Adrian: Jeff.

Jeff: But I liked him.

Adrian: Jeff.

Jeff: I was his bodyguard in school.

Adrian: Jeff.

Jeff: Fought off all the bullies who wanted to hurt him.

Adrian: Jeff.

Jeff: And he's had a soft spot for me ever since.

Adrian: Jeff.

Jeff: He was really angry when he found out I was dating Cathy.

Adrian: Jeff.

Jeff: But when we broke up, Ade forgave me.

Adrian: Jeff.

Jeff: I like Ade.

Adrian: Jeff.

Jeff: He's a swell guy.

Adrian: Oh, Jeff.

*(**Adrian** steps off platform. Slow, dream-like music starts. Polarity: **Adrian** pulls **Jeff**'s arms up, then runs his arms down **Jeff**'s torso until they rest on his hips. **Jeff** and **Adrian** turn, **Jeff** pushes **Adrian** away. **Adrian** grabs arm, shakes it. Their arms lock. **Jeff** pushes **Adrian** down on his knees. They embrace and detach.)*

Jeff: Hey, man.

Adrian: Hey.

Jeff: How's life?

Adrian: Not bad.

(Pause.)

Adrian: I'm sorry.

Jeff: *(Sits on platform.)* About what?

Adrian: Things.

Jeff: What things?

ADRIAN: You and Cathy.

JEFF: Will you get off it?

ADRIAN: What?

JEFF: That's all you ever talk about.

ADRIAN: But I *am* sorry.

JEFF: It's no big deal.

ADRIAN: I'm sorry.

JEFF: Just forget about it.

(Pause.)

ADRIAN: Jeff.

JEFF: What?

ADRIAN: Got a cigarette?

JEFF: Sure.

ADRIAN: *(Crosses to JEFF.)* Thanks.

JEFF: Let me light it for you.

ADRIAN: Thanks.

(ADRIAN sits beside JEFF. JEFF lights ADRIAN's cigarette. Pause.)

Jeff.

JEFF: What?

ADRIAN: I like your socks.

JEFF: What?

ADRIAN: Your socks.

JEFF: My socks?

ADRIAN: Yeah.

JEFF: Thanks.

(Pause.)

ADRIAN: Jeff?

JEFF: What?

ADRIAN: Can I talk to you about something?

JEFF: Sure big guy. What?

(Silence.)

ADRIAN: Jeff.

(Silence. ***ADRIAN*** *touches* ***JEFF****'s arm.)*

JEFF: Don't.

(Silence.)

ADRIAN: Jeff, please.

JEFF: *(Scared.)* No!

ADRIAN: *(Touches **JEFF**'s thigh.)* I have to say it.

JEFF: *(Stands up.)* Get the fuck away from me!

*(**JEFF** exits the light.)*

ADRIAN: Jeff!

*(**CATHY**, stage right; **ADRIAN**, centre; **JEFF**, stage left. Pools of light on all of them. All face the audience. Sound of a clock ticking.)*

CATHY: It is ten minutes to two. Early Sunday morning.

JEFF: I can't sleep.

CATHY: I can't sleep.

JEFF: I've missed two weeks of work.

CATHY: This headache is killing me.

JEFF: And it won't go away.

CATHY: It's like a fever, I tell you.

JEFF: Throbbing.

CATHY: Burning.

JEFF: No girl should mean this much.

CATHY: Why didn't I just say it?

JEFF: Christ, what about Ade?

CATHY: I didn't have the guts.

JEFF: He's my best friend.

CATHY: God, I have to say it.

JEFF: Fuck, I have to say it.

CATHY: Jeff.

JEFF: Cathy.

JEFF & CATHY: *(Together.)* Adrian.

ADRIAN: I like your socks.

(Lights on JEFF *and* CATHY*. The clock continues to tick. Accelerando. Crescendo.)*

JEFF: It is five minutes to two. Early Sunday morning.

CATHY: Jeff.

JEFF: I'm gonna phone him.

CATHY: Adrian.

JEFF: I owe him that.

CATHY: Somebody.

JEFF: But he'll think I'm a fag.

CATHY: Just say it.

JEFF: I'm going over to Cathy's.

(Light on ADRIAN.)

ADRIAN: I'm just really old-fashioned.

JEFF: Right now.

CATHY: I wish I'd never met you.

ADRIAN: I like your socks.

JEFF: I'm here.

CATHY: Fuck both of you.

ADRIAN: I like your teacups.

JEFF: I'm gonna tell her.

CATHY: You make me puke.

ADRIAN: I like the designs.

JEFF: Knock.

CATHY: I'm so lonely.

ADRIAN: The flowers.

JEFF: Just knock.

CATHY: I'm so lonely.

ADRIAN: The butterflies.

JEFF: I can't.

CATHY: I'm so fucking lonely.

ADRIAN: The vomit.

JEFF: You've got no guts.

CATHY: Just say it.

ADRIAN: I'm just really old-fashioned.

JEFF: Who asked you?

CATHY: Who asked you?

ADRIAN: Who the fuck asked you?

JEFF: Swallow it.

CATHY: Swallow it.

ADRIAN: Swallow your fucking pride.

JEFF: I need you.

ADRIAN: I need you.

CATHY: Both of you.

ADRIAN: Both of you.

CATHY: Jeff.

ADRIAN: Oh, Jeff.

JEFF: Cathy.

ADRIAN: Oh, Cathy.

CATHY: Adrian.

JEFF: Hey, big guy!

CATHY: Say it!

ADRIAN: Both of you!

JEFF: I can't!

ADRIAN: I like your socks.

CATHY: Jeff!

ADRIAN: I WANT YOU!

JEFF: Cathy!

ADRIAN: I WANT YOU!

CATHY: Adrian!

JEFF: HEY BIG GUY!

CATHY: SAY IT!

ADRIAN: BOTH OF YOU!

JEFF: I CAN'T!

ADRIAN: I… LIKE… YOUR… SOCKS…

(Sound of glass shattering.)

CATHY: Who's there?

ADRIAN: *(Blood-red light on him.)* Shut up!

CATHY: Adrian!

ADRIAN: SHUT UP!

CATHY: *(Terrified, simulating a physical struggle.)* NO... NO... NO!

*(Silence. **CATHY** falls to the ground, sobbing, singing very slowly.)*

"Bring back, bring back, oh, bring back my bonny to me, to me; Bring back, bring back, oh, bring back my bonny to me."

(Silence.)

ADRIAN: Jeff.

JEFF: Cathy.

Cathy: Adrian.

(Pause.)

Adrian: Say it.

Jeff: Somebody.

Cathy: Say it.

(Pause.)

Adrian: I love you.

(Pause.)

Jeff: I love you.

(Pause.)

Cathy: I love you.

*(Lights down. **Cathy** and **Jeff** exit.)*

*Nelson Wong as **Jeff**, Ntsikie Kheswa as **Cathy**, and Thrasso Petras as **Adrian** in "Motifs & Repetitions." Photo by Mélissa C. Powell.*

Scene 3

(The clock strikes twelve. Images of skyscrapers and buildings appear on the left and right scrims. City sounds crescendo to fff in the darkness.)

Adrian: Down.
Down.
DOWN!

*(The city sounds decrescendo to p. **Adrian**'s voice is calmer.)*

Light.

*(Light on **Adrian**. He is facing the audience. Both **Adrian**'s voice and the city sounds crescendo as the speech progresses. The tempo is fast.)*

You're my city, this is my show, you're my city, this is my show, so you know why I was facing upstage in the first scene? It's 'cause of this, *(points at chest) this*, you can't see it now but I possess a huge black hole in my chest and I love it, I love it, but I don't show it off, I'm always fully clothed, even when I fuck, but I love it, I love it, it can stretch *this* wide and it's clear as the night sky and when you lean over and look down you see nothing, *nothing*, it's a bottomless pit, no end in sight and if you drop something in it you'll never see it again, like my dog, my Chihuahua, that I loved more than life, he leapt into it one day and I haven't seen him since, I've lost a lot of things in this huge black hole—my dog, my watch, my bracelet, my mother—but I don't care I still love it, it's mine and I love it, the only thing I hate is the jazz, the jazz, the jazz it plays all night every night, the jazz from my hole all night fast as light

(The city sounds reach fff.)

Down.
Down.
DOWN!

(The city sounds decrescendo to p. ***Adrian*** *exits. Lights out.)*

Thrasso Petras as ***Adrian*** *in "Ticks."*

Scene 4

Adrian: *(Offstage.)* Light.

(Beat.)

On Cathy.

*(Light on **Cathy**, behind a chair.)*

Brighter.

(Light brightens.)

One.

Cathy: Light.
Light.
Through blinds.
On cheek.
Nimbus of light invades room.
Reveals nothing.
But the dark.

Adrian: *(Offstage.)* Light.

*(Light out on **Cathy**.)*

Cathy, stage left, eyeing hand. Light.

*(Light on **Cathy**, stage left, sitting on chair, eyeing hand.)*

Two.

Cathy: Hands.
Fingers.
Each one pointing to the sky.
Elm trees in winter. Arthritic.
No cure.
No spring.

Adrian: *(Offstage.)* Light.

*(Light out on **Cathy**.)*

Cathy, up centre, stroking hair. Light.

*(Light on **Cathy**, up centre, sitting on platform, stroking hair, rocking back and forth.)*

Three.

Cathy: *(Quoting Samuel Hoffenstein.)* "Babies haven't any hair;
Old men's heads are just as bare;
Between the cradle and the grave
Lies a haircut and a shave."
Had my hair done today.

Had it styled. No. *Coiffed.*
My hair used to go to my shins,
In the days before I knew... I was alive.

Adrian: *(Offstage.)* Light.

(Light out on **Cathy.***)*

Cathy, stage right. Light.

(Light on **Cathy***, stage right, sitting on chair.)*

Four.

Cathy: Just this afternoon I had eyebrows.
Then suddenly, I thought, What the hell.
I want my eyebrows to be what I say.
I want canopies.
Wings.

Adrian: *(Offstage.)* Light.

(Light out on **Cathy.***)*

Cathy, down centre, legs spread. Light.

(Light on **Cathy***, down centre, legs spread.)*

Five.

Cathy: I met someone.
Last night.
On the street.

A man.
No one special. Just a man. With a smile.
Teeth shining.
In the dark.

ADRIAN: *(Offstage.)* Light.

(Light out on **CATHY**.*)*

Cathy, up centre, clutching chest. Light.

(Light on **CATHY**, *up centre, sitting on platform.)*

Six.

CATHY: What happened to that old diamond brooch?
What happened to that old diamond brooch?

ADRIAN: *(Offstage.)* Light.

(Light out on **CATHY**.*)*

Cathy, stage left, eyeing hand. Light.

(Light on **CATHY**, *stage left, standing in front of chair, wringing hands, fidgeting nervously.)*

Seven.

CATHY: Every once in a while I dream of spring.
Music strings of pearls from my hands.
No, not pearls. Diamonds.
Music strings of diamonds from my hands.

Mozart streaming from my fingers.
Filling the silence of the room.
Now all is quiet. Dark.
So I listen...to *my* dream...of spring.

ADRIAN: *(Offstage.)* Light.

(Light out on CATHY.*)*

Cathy, up centre, stroking hair. Light.

(Light on CATHY*, up centre, sitting on platform, stroking hair.)*

Eight.

CATHY: My hair was five feet long.
Straight.
Blonde.
No, not blonde. Flaxen.
Straight flaxen hair to my shins.
I never—ever—wore it up.
Down it all went. A waterfall.

ADRIAN: *(Offstage.)* Light.

(Light out on CATHY.*)*

Cathy, stage right. Light.

(Light on CATHY*, stage right, sitting on chair.)*

Nine.

Cathy: It's not that my eyebrows were ugly.
I groomed them as well as I could.
You might say they were a tad too hairy.
No, not hairy. *Pilose.*
But I trimmed them. Three nights a week.
10:45 PM.
Tweezers so cold against skin.

Adrian: *(Offstage.)* Light.

(Light out on **Cathy**.*)*

Cathy, down centre, legs spread. Light.

(Light on **Cathy**, *down centre, on the floor, legs spread.)*

Ten.

Cathy: I can't say I remember what he looks like.
Everything seemed so dark.
All I remember are his teeth.
Teeth milk-white in the night.
Slowly, the teeth came towards me.
The hand inched forward. Beckoned.
No tired lines, no clichés.
"You," he said. "Come."

Adrian: *(Offstage.)* Light.

(Light out on **Cathy**.*)*

Cathy, centre, clutching chest. Light.

(Light on **Cathy***, centre, standing in front of the chair.)*

Eleven.

Cathy: *(Looking upward, as though confronting* **Adrian***'s voice.)* What happened to that old diamond brooch?
That brooch I showed off like a child.
Of course, the diamonds weren't real.
But how they shone like stars in the dark.

Adrian: *(Offstage.)* Light.

(Light out on **Cathy***.)*

Voices.

*(***Cathy 2***,* **Cathy 3***,* **Cathy 4***, and* **Cathy 5** *enter one by one, wearing white masks. They deliver their lines with no inflection or emotion.)*

Cathy 2: *(Sits on chair.)* Elms.
Winter.
Mozart.
Spring.

Cathy 3: *(Stands on platform.)* Cradle.
Grave.
Cut.
Coiffed.

Cathy 4: *(Sits on chair.)* Hairy.
Pilose.
Canopies.

Wings.

Cathy 5: *(Sits down centre, legs spread.)* Smile.
Teeth.
Dark.

Cathy 2, 3, 4 & 5: *(Together.)* Light.

Cathy: Light.
Light.
Through blinds.
On cheek.
Nimbus of light invades room.
Reveals nothing.
But the dark.

Cathy 2: Elm trees in winter.

Cathy 3: Had my hair done today.

Cathy 4: Canopies. Wings.

Cathy 5: Just a man. With a smile.

Cathy 2: No cure.

Cathy 3: No, *coiffed.*

Cathy 4: No, *pilose.*

Cathy 5: No clichés.

Cathy 2: Hands.

Cathy 3: Hair.

Cathy 4: Brows.

Cathy 2, 3, 4 & 5: *(Together.)* Light.

Cathy: Light.
Light.
Through blinds.
On cheek.
Nimbus of light invades room.
Reveals nothing.
But the dark.

Cathy 2: Stiff, knotted hands on keys.

Cathy 3: How strange to find out I'm alive.

Cathy 4: How fine this pencil in my hands.

Cathy 5: "You," he said. "Come."

Cathy 2: Slowly, the frost begins to melt.

Cathy 3: My hair to the ground like vines.

Cathy 4: How black this pencil in my hands.

Cathy 5: "You," he said. "Come."

Cathy 2: My thumb thumps out the first note.

Cathy 3: High time it was to be alive.

CATHY 4: How sharp this pencil in my hands.

CATHY 5: "You," he said. "Come."

CATHY 2: The flight of fingers in spring.

CATHY 3: Snip, snip, the power was mine.

CATHY 4: Wings, give me life.

CATHY 5: "You," he said. "Come."
So glaring the whiteness of teeth.
So swift the walk over bridge.
So cold the night air on my face.
The warmth of the hand gripping mine.
So quick the turn of the knob.
So loud the closing of door.
So painful the fingers in my hair.
The *life* of the tongue on my mouth.

CATHY 2: The frost refuses to melt.

CATHY 3: My hair lies dead on the floor.

CATHY 4: Wings for arms, a butterfly's.

CATHY 5: "Diamonds," I said. "Diamonds."

CATHY 2: Elm trees bare against sky.

CATHY 3: The end of a life without light.

CATHY 4: Wings for arms, an eagle's.

CATHY 5: "Diamonds," I said. "Diamonds."

CATHY 2: The house is submerged in snow.

CATHY 3: A hairy old hag no more.

CATHY 4: Wings for arms, to the sky.

CATHY 5: "Diamonds," I said. "Diamonds."

CATHY 2: But the music continues to play.

CATHY 3: My hair is finally mine.

CATHY 4: Wings for arms, to the sun.

CATHY 5: "Diamonds," I said. "Diamonds."

(CATHY stands, goes over to CATHY 5, puts her hands on the latter's shoulders. She whispers CATHY 5's lines along with her.)

So hard.
So deep.
So warm.
So wet.
Fast as a falling star.
Diamonds.
Diamonds.

CATHY: Light.
Light.
Down from a golden sun.
I listen...to *my* dream...of spring...
Can you see me?
Can you?

(Singing defiantly.) "Bring back, bring back,
Oh bring back my bonny to me, to me.
Bring back, bring back,
Oh bring back my bonny to me."

*(As soon as **Cathy** begins to sing, **Cathy 2**, **Cathy 3**, **Cathy 4**, and **Cathy 5** exit with chairs. When she is done singing, **Cathy** follows.)*

*Michael Fera as **Cathy 4**, Tanja Dixon-Warren as **Cathy 5**, Ntsikie Kheswa as **Cathy**, and Nelson Wong as **Cathy 3** in "Diamond." Photo by Mélissa C. Powell.*

Scene 5

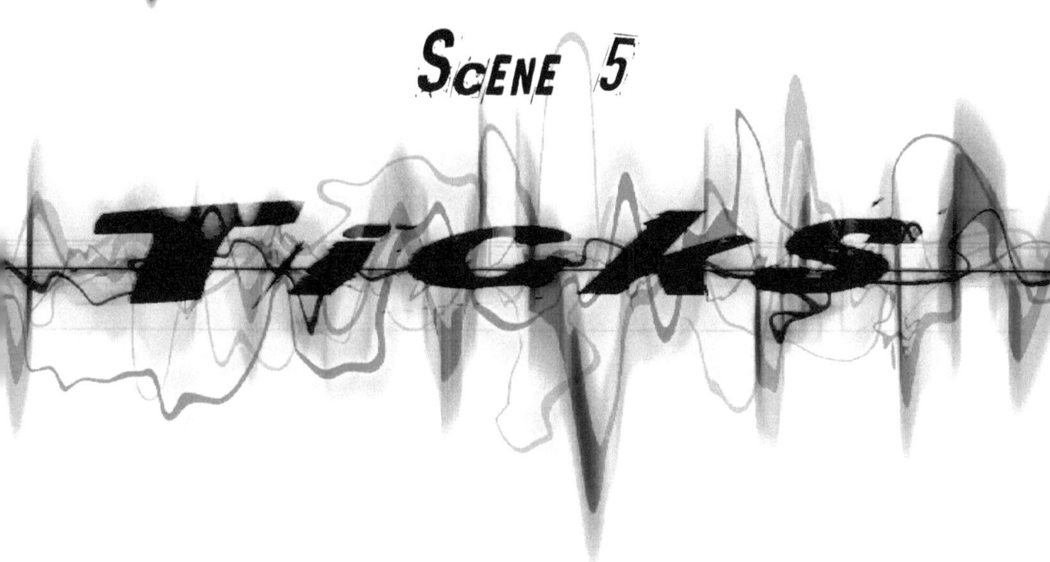

Adrian: Light.

(Light on **Adrian***. He faces the audience. Both his voice and the city sounds crescendo as the speech progresses. The tempo is fast.)*

Adrian: *(Pacing.)* You're my city, this is my show, you're my city, this is my show, so you know why I was facing upstage in the first scene?, it's 'cause of this, *(points at chest) this*, you can't see it now but I possess a huge black hole in my chest and I love it, I love it, but I don't show it off, I'm always fully clothed, even when I fuck, but I love it, I love it, so this friend of mine, okay, who I haven't seen in years, we bump into each other one day and I tell him 'bout my hole, and we agree to meet for dinner on such and such a night, and so I'm there that night but he never shows up, and this friend of mine, okay, my best friend in the world, the person to whom I first broke the news 'bout my hole, I pass her on the street and she's walking really slow, and she sees me, I know she sees me, but doesn't say a word, and this guy, okay, who, like, works in the supermarket, who I always kinda liked but never once talked to, and so I'm in there one day and we get around to talking and I tell him 'bout my hole and he throws me out of the store, and there's this girl, okay, who I really want to talk to, 'cause I just want to talk, I just *really* want to talk, so I've been phoning her every day for the last six weeks, once, twice, three times every day, but when I phone she's never home so I've been leaving her messages, giving her the info on the beauty of my hole, but she's never phoned back until today when she finally said, LOOK I'VE GOT NO TIME FOR YOU SO STOP PHONING ME ASSHOLE, and like night after night there's jazz from my hole, jazz from my hole all night fast as light

(The city sounds reach fff.)

Down.
Down.
DOWN!

*(The music and city sounds cut out. **Adrian** exits.)*

*Thrasso Petras as **Adrian** in "Ticks."*

Scene 6

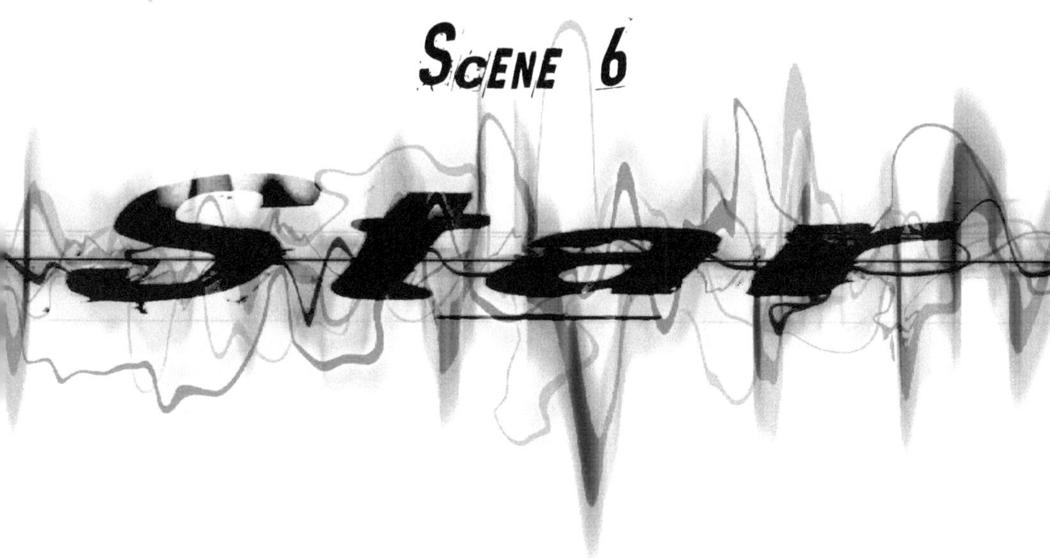

(Jeff enters stage left with a laundry basket full of props.)

Jeff: Kleenex.

(Moves behind bed.)

Linen.

(Adjusts linen on bed.)

Walls and bed milk-white.
Silk-smooth teddy polar bear.

(Takes tissue, sits on bed, feigns wiping tears.)

Tears down cheek like lard.
Little sister Myra.
Little Miss Miami.
Diamonds God-white stars in dark.
Dimpled thank-you smile.

(Gets up from bed.)

"Hey, big brother, don't smoke inside the house."

(Crosses behind bed.)

Morning eyes bright berry-blue.
Star-round tray.
Out.
"Hey, big brother, give me back my teddy."
Morning lips sweet ketchup-red.
Snow-cold shower.
Stoplight.
Moon-kissed scalp,

(Takes off shirt.)

Star of gold.
Face as mild as cream.
Hair like tuft, lemon-light.
Stars ablaze mouth-ends.
Stars 'round head, gift of wings.

(Takes off pants.)

Flowers wet with joy.

(Takes off underwear.)

Brother happy, mouth a-drip.

(Sits on bed.)

Queen afloat throne-bed.

(Climbs under the linens.)

Baby queen.
Lily queen.
Hand silk lace 'round stems.
Light through blinds, optic trick.
Hand not silk but snake.
Next to you, finger face.
Spit down throat like milk.
Fingers brown... down arms... milk-white...
Snake... twines... snake... night's... end...

(Comes. Pause. Sits up, faces up stage, gets out of bed. Puts on dressing gown. From under bed, pulls out box. Withdraws blonde wig. Wears it. Diamond tiara. Wears it. Sits on the front of bed, pulls hand mirror from box, looks at himself.)

(Smiling.) Sister.
Sister.
Star o'er high white hill.
Tearstained cheeks, baby-white.

(JEFF picks up the azaleas.)

Hot milk up sweet thighs.

(Sound of people applauding as JEFF crosses to stage left, pool of light on him. He basks in the spotlight, places the azaleas in a vase, then exits.)

Nelson Wong as **Jeff** *in "Star."*

Scene 7

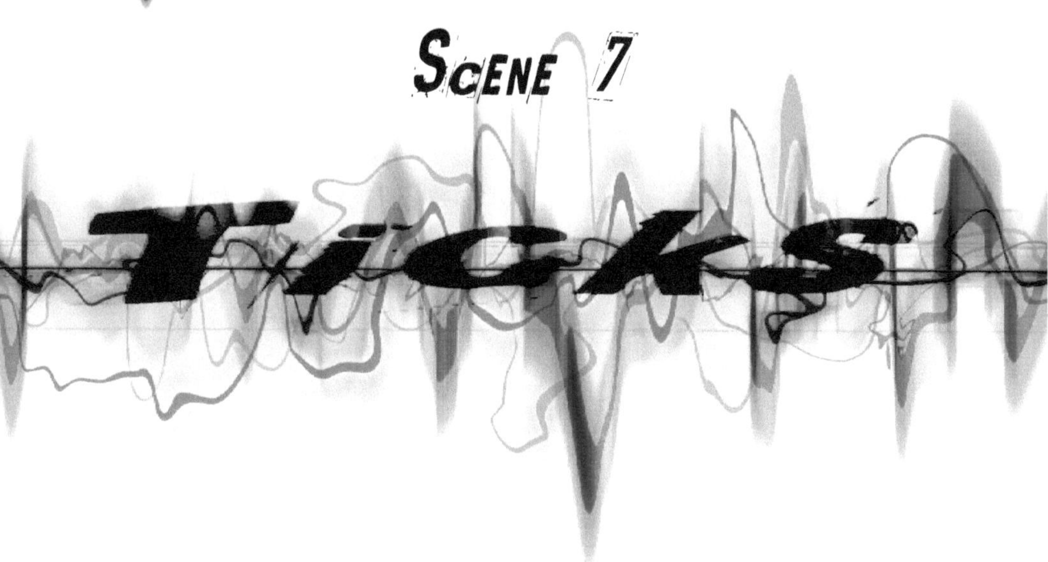

Adrian: Light.

*(**Philip** and **Mary** enter, **Philip** with a chair and newspaper. **Philip** sits on the chair and reads the paper. **Mary** on the chaise. Tableau. **Adrian** crosses to behind the table and stands beside **Mary**. He delivers this section more slowly and less frantically than the previous ones.)*

You're my city, this is my show, you're my city, this is my show.

So you know why I was facing upstage in the first scene? It's 'cause of this, *(Points at chest.) this.* You can't see it now but I possess a huge black hole in my chest and I love it, I love it, but I don't show it off, I'm always fully clothed, even when I fuck *(Looks at **Philip.**)*. But I love it, I love it. 'Cause it makes you more honest. The hole is the truth—the hole is the Word.

(ADRIAN sits on the corner of the table, near MARY.)

Like this guy I know, okay, the most selfish prick I'd ever met, never heard a word you said 'less it had something to do with him. But after he got his hole he actually learned to *listen*. Now he's a sponge, he can *feel* everything you say.

And this girl I know, okay, fucking vain as Scarlett O'Hara, all she cared about were her Gucci bags, her lip gloss and her split ends. But since she got her hole she's been feeding kids on the streets of Calcutta, her hole is fucking expansive *(He moves centre stage.)*, can take the whole world in.

Now when was the last time you gave some change to a beggar? When was the last time you actually looked at one in the eye? When was the last time you really listened to your friends? When was the last time you put someone's needs ahead of your own? When was the last time you thanked God for being alive? When was the last time you had the guts to admit you're weak? 'Cause we're all weak, you know, we're all in the same boat, we all want to connect, we all want to escape. And that's the only reason we have these holes in our chests—we just wanted to connect, we just wanted to escape.

So don't look at us like that, we're *in* you and *of* you, we all want something more than the jazz, the jazz from the club all night fast as light…

(The city sounds reach fff.)

Down.
Down.
DOWN!

*(The music and city sounds cut out. **Adrian** exits.)*

*Thrasso Petras as **Adrian** in "Ticks."*

Scene 8

*(**Mary** is folding clothes. She pulls a cut-out newspaper article from her apron pocket, looks at it.)*

Mary: Philip.

Philip: Mary.

Mary: *(Folding the article and putting it back in her apron pocket.)* Happy anniversary, Philip.

Philip: What?

Mary: Happy anniversary.

Philip: Why do you say it that way?

Mary: What way?

Philip: As if you thought I'd forgotten.

Mary: What are you talking about?

Philip: I didn't forget.

Mary: I didn't think you did.

Philip: I did not forget.

Mary: Did I say you did? *(Pause.)* Philip.

Philip: Mary.

Mary: Guess who I ran into the other day.

Philip: Anne Barrie.

Mary: How did you know?

Philip: I just guessed.

Mary: Guessed?

Philip: Yes.

Mary: Yes. I saw Anne Barrie the other day. It's been aeons since I last saw her. She invited me to her house and we had a long, wonderful chat. She's as radiant as ever.

Philip: Yes.

Mary: The kids are off to college. John Junior's engaged to be married.

Philip: *(Paper down.)* And John?

Mary: Engaged to be married.

Philip: Senior.

Mary: Senior?

Philip: Yes.

Mary: I don't know. He wasn't there.

Philip: *(Paper back up.)* Oh.

Mary: No. But Anne was as radiant as ever. They've redecorated the house since the last time we visited. Anne told me she was so sick of that house that after the kids moved out she wanted to sell it. But John refused, and after ferocious debate she agreed to stay as long as they could redecorate it. Oh, Philip, you should have seen their new wallpaper. The most gorgeous floral design I'd ever seen.

Philip: Yes.

Mary: A flurry of azaleas on a burgundy backdrop.

Philip: Yes.

Mary: I thought it was wonderful. It made the house seem warm.

Philip: It made the house seem dark.

Mary: You weren't there. How would you know?

Philip: Because I know. I just know.

Mary: It made it warm.

Philip: Dark.

Mary: Warm! *(Pause.)* It made it warm. *(Pause.)* As a matter of fact I'd like to get the same kind of wallpaper myself.

Philip: *(Paper down.)* You will do no such thing. I like the walls bare. *(Paper up.)* White.

Mary: Yes, Philip.

Philip: Simplicity.

Mary: Yes, Philip. *(Pause.)* Anne was as radiant as ever.

Philip: Yes.

(Pause.)

Mary: Philip.

(Pause.)

Philip: I didn't forget.

Mary: Forget what?

Philip: Our anniversary.

Mary: I never said you did.

Philip: I am not a stupid man.

Mary: I never said you were. *(Pause.)* You should have seen Anne Barrie's kitchen. It was as clean and spotless as ever. So clean you could practically eat breakfast off it.

Philip: Yes, Mary.

Mary: Anne is an incredible homemaker.

Philip: Not unlike yourself, Mary.

Mary: Do you think so?

Philip: Yes, Mary.

Mary: You're not just saying that.

Philip: No, Mary.

Mary: I try, my darling.

Philip: Yes, Mary.

Mary: I *do* try.

Philip: Yes, Mary.

Mary: But it's so difficult sometimes.

Philip: I know, Mary.

Mary: But I *do* try.

Philip: Yes, Mary.

Mary: Please believe me.

PHILIP: Yes, Mary.

(Pause.)

MARY: *(Crosses to* ***PHILIP****, kneels.)* Philip.

PHILIP: Yes.

MARY: Give me your hand.

PHILIP: My what?

MARY: Your hand, darling. Your hand. *(She reaches for* ***PHILIP****'s hand. Beat. He gives it to her.)* This may surprise you, but it was your hands that first attracted me to you.

PHILIP: Really.

MARY: We shook hands. It was so strong, your handshake, so *certain.* I knew after that that I didn't want to be with anyone else. *(She kisses his hand.)* Philip.

PHILIP: Yes.

MARY: About the wallpaper.

PHILIP: *(Pulls his hand away.)* There will be no wallpaper.

MARY: But Philip—

PHILIP: I like the walls bare.

MARY: Yes.

Philip: White.

Mary: Yes. *(Pause.)* Philip.

Philip: Yes.

Mary: Put your paper down.

Philip: What?

Mary: *(With some anger, stands up.)* Put your paper down.

Philip: I don't think I will.

*(Pause. **Mary** snatches paper from **Philip**, throws it on the floor.)*

Mary: *(Crosses to stage right.)* Guess what I found.

Philip: I don't appreciate your doing that.

Mary: GUESS WHAT I FOUND.

Philip: HOW DARE YOU DO THAT.

Mary: Guess what I found in the basement this morning.

(From her apron pocket she withdraws a pair of mittens.)

Junior's mittens. You remember, don't you? *(She crosses to stage left.)* The mittens I made for him for his sixth birthday. Or was it Christmas? Yes, it was Christmas. Yes. His birthday and Christmas are only a month apart—that's why I keep getting them mixed up.

It was the year we first discovered his incredible talent, remember? The year that professor at the academy declared him a prodigy. So I simply had to make him new mittens, to protect those hands of his from the cold. He has beautiful hands. He has *beautiful* hands.

Philip: Has?

Mary: Yes.

Philip: The present tense?

(Pause.)

Mary: Let's not get into this. *(Crosses to stage right.)*

Philip: We agreed never to speak of him in the present tense.

Mary: Let's not get into this.

Philip: He *had* beautiful hands.

Mary: Let's just forget it, all right?

Philip: HE *HAD* BEAUTIFUL HANDS. *(Pause. Calmly.)* He *had* beautiful hands, just like his father—that is until his mother pushed him into piano lessons and made moth wings out of them.

Mary: He had talent!

Philip: His hands were never meant to unfold! *(He raises his fist.)* His hands were never meant to unfold. But they did. Just like that. *(On "that" he snaps his fingers.)* And he proved himself incompetent.

MARY: He is *not* incompetent.

PHILIP: Is?

MARY: He is a prodigy.

PHILIP: Is?

MARY: He is our son.

PHILIP: Is? *(Beat.)* Is? Is? Is? *(Pause.)* Shut up if you insist on speaking of him in the present tense.

*(**PHILIP** turns away, looks stage left. Silence. **MARY** crosses to couch, sits, recovers, folds clothes.)*

MARY: Anne Barrie... she's such an expert homemaker.

PHILIP: Not unlike yourself, Mary.

MARY: Do you think so?

PHILIP: Yes, Mary.

MARY: You're not just saying that?

PHILIP: No, Mary.

MARY: I *do* try. Really. I *do* try.

PHILIP: Yes, Mary.

Mary: *(On the verge of tears, hugging him.)* I *do* try, my darling. Please believe me.

Philip: Yes, Mary.

Mary: Please believe me!

(Silence.)

Philip: So you like my hands, do you?

Mary: Very much, Philip.

Philip: I'm not the least bit surprised. I like them myself.

Mary: They're so strong.

Philip: Yes.

Mary: They have a certain…rough beauty.

(Pause.)

Philip: When I was a boy, I was a very bad boy. Every time I pulled a stunt my father would have me hold my hand out and he'd take a whip to it, five strikes of the whip—one, two, three, four, five *(He stands.)*—five strikes of the whip and nothing else, just the whip my great-grandfather had left my grandfather had left my father. And you know what? It thrilled me. I was mesmerized by the rhythm, the rhythm of it all, the motion, the controlled motion of his hand—he had beautiful hands—the curve of that whip falling flat on my palm, the blue vein of determination popping out between his brows, the sweat oozing from his temples, the glorious glow in his beautiful eyes. I needed it, I knew I needed it, despite the pain, oh the pain, but it was necessary. It was right. And it gave me a thrill.

MARY: A thrill?

PHILIP: It was all… for the sake of… simplicity. *(Pause.)* Could you retrieve my paper, please? *(He sits.)*

MARY: *(Stands, crosses to* ***PHILIP****.)* Of course, Philip. *(She picks up paper, gives it to* ***PHILIP****. Pause.)* Philip.

PHILIP: *(Reading the paper again.)* What?

MARY: *(Hesitantly.)* Aren't you tired of this house?

PHILIP: *(Paper down.)* What?

MARY: This house. Aren't you tired of it?

PHILIP: Why do you ask that?

MARY: Please don't be angry…

PHILIP: … how dare you even suggest that…

MARY: … but it's been something I've been meaning to ask you…

PHILIP: HOW DARE YOU ASK THAT.

MARY: Please, darling, just listen to me.

PHILIP: We've lived in this house for twenty-five years and I have no intention of ever leaving it. Is that clear?

Mary: Philip, please—

Philip: IS THAT CLEAR?

*(Pause. **Philip** returns to his newspaper.)*

Mary: Philip?

Philip: What?

Mary: *(Crosses behind chaise.)* I… I think we have to do something about this house. Every morning I sit in this room, my hands folded in my lap, and I see this table, this vase of azaleas, these chairs, these walls. I will sit here motionless for hours on end, trying to see more than what is here. But I can't. *(Crosses in front of chaise.)* I can't live like this, darling—it's tearing me apart. One day you'll walk in on me and I'll be cutting my skin open with the broken pieces of this vase. *(Sits on chaise.)* Have you been listening to me?

(Pause.)

Philip: If you want to leave me, Mary, no one's stopping you. *(Pause.)* If you hate this house so much, just leave. Go on. LEAVE!

(Silence.)

Mary: *(Stands, crosses to stage right down, talking as if simply for the hell of it, once again taking mittens out of apron pocket.)* These mittens. They were Junior's, remember? I found them while I was rummaging in the basement this morning. Christmas, wasn't it? Yes, Christmas, of course, Christmas. I gave them to him when he was six years old. How small his hands were. How big they are now.

Philip: Are?

Mary: Yes.

Philip: Why do you use the present tense?

(Pause.)

Mary: Because… I want to.

Philip: I thought we agreed never to speak of him in the present tense.

Mary: I think I've forgotten the exact reason why we shouldn't.

Philip: *(Folds paper up, tosses it on the table.)* Well perhaps I should remind you.

Mary: Well perhaps you should.

(Pause.)

Philip: He failed us, Mary…

Mary: He has not failed us…

Philip: … he nearly brought this house down…

Mary: … you're just imagining things…

Philip: … he *wanted* to bring this house down…

Mary: … this is absolute nonsense…

Philip: … but you know what? He didn't! He couldn't! I saved our souls and I saved this house from the rage of that disgusting pervert.

Mary: Anne Barrie is as radiant as ever. She redid the walls—did I tell you that? *(Crosses to chaise.)* With the most gorgeous floral design I've ever seen.

Mary: *(Sits on the chaise.)* I think wallpaper would do wonders for our house, don't you?

Philip: I saved this house, Mary, and don't you forget it.

Mary: Our walls have been bare for too long now, don't you think?

Philip: I stood my ground. I saved us both.

Mary: They're practically screaming for cover.

Philip: He's dead.

Mary: We're going to get exactly the same kind of wallpaper the Barries have.

Philip: He's dead.

Mary: I'll start first thing in the morning.

(She crosses to centre stage. ***Philip*** *stands in her way.)*

Philip: He's dead.

Mary: I'm going to the kitchen.

Philip: You're not going anywhere.

Mary: I have to make you coffee.

Philip: You wanted to talk about him and that's exactly what we're going to do.

Mary: Philip, please—

Philip: He's dead.

Mary: He's not dead.

Philip: He is dead.

Mary: *(Crosses to stage right.)* He is *not* dead!

Philip: But we must go on living as if he were.

Mary: He is *not* dead! He's coming home this afternoon!

(Pause.)

Philip: He is *not* coming home.

Mary: Philip, he is.

Philip: You're lying!

Mary: I'm not lying!

Philip: *(In absolute terror, stepping toward* ***Mary.****)* HE IS *NOT* COMING HOME! HE IS *NOT* COMING HOME! *(Pause. He takes a deep breath, clears his throat, regains his composure.)* Why… why would he come home, after all that's happened?

Mary: *What's* happened?

Philip: Oh, Mary, you really are testing my patience today, you know that?

Mary: I haven't the slightest idea what you're talking about.

(Silence.)

Philip: Our child… our only child… is a degenerate.

(Silence.)

Mary: He is not… that.

(Pause.)

Philip: Oh, Mary, he told us right to our face.

(Pause.)

Mary: It was a lie! It was just a silly story he made up!

(Pause.)

Philip: Mary, get this straight: he's dead.

Mary: No!

Philip: He died the day he walked out that door! And nothing will ever change that.

*(Silence. **Philip** returns to chair. **Mary**, visibly shaken, crosses to chaise, sits, starts folding laundry again.)*

Mary: Guess who I ran into the other day.

Philip: Anne Barrie.

Mary: How did you know?

Philip: I just guessed.

Mary: Anne was as radiant as ever. John Jr.'s engaged to be married.

Philip: And John?

Mary: Engaged to be married.

Philip: Senior.

Mary: Senior.

Philip: Yes.

Mary: Oh. *(Pause.)* I don't know. He wasn't there.

Philip: He wasn't there.

Mary: No.

Philip: It *has* been a long time since we last saw them, hasn't it?

Mary: Yes.

Philip: The four of us used to be so close.

Mary: Yes.

Philip: We used to spend all our weekends with them.

Mary: Yes.

Philip: They'd come to our place or we'd go to theirs.

Mary: Yes.

Philip: But for some reason we just drifted apart.

Mary: Yes.

Philip: They stopped calling us and we stopped calling them.

Mary: Yes.

Philip: It's too bad. I'm beginning to miss them. *(Beat.)* It *has* been a long time since we last saw them.

Mary: Yes.

Philip: I've known John since I was a kid.

Mary: Yes.

Philip: I think he was always very fond of you.

MARY: Was he?

PHILIP: I was never really sure what you thought of him.

MARY: Not much.

PHILIP: Not much?

MARY: I never cared for him.

PHILIP: No?

MARY: No.

(Pause.)

PHILIP: The four of us used to be so close.

MARY: Yes.

PHILIP: All those weekends we spent with them.

MARY: Yes.

PHILIP: All the fun things we did with them.

MARY: Yes.

PHILIP: Camping.

MARY: Yes.

PHILIP: Eating.

Mary: Yes.

Philip: Swinging.

(Pause.)

Mary: What?

Philip: Oh, yes. That's right. I forgot.

(Pause.)

I took a rain check. Anne's a dog.

(Silence.)

Mary: I really must make your coffee now.

*(Pause. **Mary** does not leave.)*

Philip: Mary. Really. There's no use hiding. It's all out in the open now. *(**Mary** cries.)* Oh, Mary, really. There's no use crying. I knew about you and John a long time ago. Believe me, I understand. These things happen. I saw the two of you fucking but I took it in stride. Really, Mary, you must stop crying. Because no matter what you do, nothing will ever change. Our house will remain as it is.

*(**Philip** returns to his newspaper. **Mary** is trembling.)*

Mary: Philip.

Philip: Mary.

Mary: John and I called it off a long time ago.

Philip: Really, Mary, there's no need to explain.

Mary: *(**Mary** crosses to **Philip**.)* I never meant to hurt you.

Philip: Of course not.

Mary: Please forgive me.

Philip: I already have.

Mary: *(Kneeling before him.)* I never meant to—

Philip: Be quiet.

Mary: But Philip—

Philip: *(Paper down.)* BE QUIET! *(Pause. Very calmly.)* I'm on the edge, Mary. Just on the edge. I'm fifty-one years old, and I've learned to believe what I want to believe. *(Paper up, but not covering face.)* Right now I'm making myself believe that you're the girl I married twenty-five years ago, not the haggard old baggage you are now. But I'm also prepared to forget about your little thing with John Barrie, and simply chuckle at the idea of any man not fully off his rocker even thinking of having an affair with you. But I *am* on the edge, Mary —*(Looks at **Mary**.)* *just* on the edge. *(**Philip**'s face hidden completely behind paper.)* So either you shut the fuck up right here and now or I'll drag you by the hair to the garage and blow your brains out. Really, Mary, it's up to you.

(Silence.)

Mary: *(Slowly rising.)* Oh, Philip… What is happening? *(Pause.)* What in hell on earth is happening?

(The doorbell rings.)

Junior? Junior?

*(**Adrian** enters. He is wearing a black leather jacket and pants, an earring, dark glasses.)*

Junior.

*(**Mary** goes to him, hugs him.)*

You're a bit early, aren't you? Philip? *(Pause.)* Philip?

*(**Philip** does not respond, continues to read the paper.)*

Don't mind him, dear. He's just tired is all. He spent the whole morning putting up new wallpaper. The living room isn't done yet. Just the bedroom... How are you? *(Silence.)* I missed you. *(Pause.)* You've… changed so much. *(Turns to **Philip** for a beat.)* Hasn't he, Philip? *(Silence.)* Let me see your hands.

*(She grabs **Adrian**'s hands.)*

Oh, how strong they are! But then they've got to be strong—you're a concert pianist, for God's sake! And your father here calls your hands moth wings! *(Beat.)* Guess what I found.

(She pulls out mittens.)

Your old mittens. Remember? I gave them to you for Christmas when you were six years old. How small your hands were. How big they are now.

*(She crosses to chaise, ushering **Adrian** in.)*

I made them for you the year that professor at the Academy declared you a prodigy. I simply had to make you new mittens, to protect those hands of yours from the cold. And you loved these mittens so much that you wore them all the time, even in the summertime. "I am a concert pianist," you'd tell those horrid boys next door. "I have to protect my hands." And they'd beat you up black and blue and you'd run to me crying, and I'd take you in my arms and tell you that everything would be all right, that when you grew up you'd stand head and shoulders above them all.

(She sits on the chaise.)

How quiet you are today. But then you've always been quiet, haven't you? You never did say much, did you? Except with your beautiful, beautiful eyes... Why do you hide your eyes under such dark, dark glasses? Take them off. Please? For me?

*(He does not. She crosses to behind **Philip**'s chair.)*

I guess you're wondering how your father and I have been doing. *(Silence.)* We've been doing fine. Haven't we, Philip? Whatever problems we may have had we've worked through and taken care of. That's because we believe in each other, and we believe in the life we've built together. Every morning I sit in this room, my hands folded in my lap, and I see this table, this vase of azaleas, these chairs, these walls. And I will sit here motionless for hours on end, thanking God for giving us the life we have.

(She crosses to behind table, stops in between chaise and table.)

We wake up. *(Beat.)* We eat breakfast. *(Beat.)* Your father goes to work. *(Beat.)* I clean the house. *(Beat.)* Your father comes home. *(Beat.)* We eat dinner. *(Beat.)* We watch some TV. *(Beat.)* We go to bed. *(Pause.)* The simplicity of it all. And we love it. Every day when the time is right I'll take his hand in mine. It's so strong, his hand, so certain. I'm the luckiest woman in the world.

(Pause. ***Mary's*** *eyes catch* ***Adrian's****, falter.)*

Why do you look at me that way? Stop it. *(Pause.)* Stop it, do you hear me? I won't have it! *(Pause.)* You're so smug. You think you've got everything figured out, don't you! Well let me tell you something: things aren't the way you think they are. We love this table, this vase of azaleas, these chairs, these walls. *(She crosses to behind* ***Philip****.)* We love this house! And we love each other! We are happy! WE ARE HAPPY!

(Silence. No reaction from ***Adrian****.)*

Is this what you came home for? To disrespect us? Is it?

(Pause.) Your father was right about you all a—My dear, can't you show me a little respect? Please? *(Pause.)* Guess what I found. Your old mittens, remember? I gave them to you for—

(She sits on chaise.)

I showed them to you already, didn't I? *(Silence.)* How's your music going? I read the reviews of your performance with the symphony the other day. They were rapturous, of course. I'm so proud of you. *(Silence.)* You *do*… wear a suit… when you perform, don't you? You look so much better in a suit. You really do. *(Pause.)* It's your father's and my anniversary today. But of course you knew that, didn't you? And no dear, he didn't forget. Your father did *not* forget. I know you'd like to think that he did but he didn't. He did *not* forget. In fact he gave me the most wonderful present he's ever given me. Wallpaper. A flurry of azaleas on a burgundy backdrop. The living room isn't done yet. Just the bedroom. *(Beat.)* All right, he hasn't put up any wallpaper, as if I can ever expect this S.O.B. to allow so much as a gob of spit to liven up this house.

*(**Adrian** laughs.)*

Don't laugh at me! Don't! Don't laugh at me! *(Beat.)* You really are having a ball, aren't you! You had this all planned before you came, didn't you! Let's have a little fun and peeve poor Mommy. Well, look at me. Look at me! Do I… look… peeved? *(Silence.)* Why did you come home? Why on earth did you come home?

*(**Adrian** stops laughing.)*

Oh, yes. I forgot. I invited you, didn't I? I invited you home… because I want you to right… a wrong. *(Beat.)* What you said about yourself… when you left… that was a lie. Wasn't it? Wasn't it? *(Beat.)* You hated this house. You *wanted* to be thrown out. That's why you made up that silly story about yourself. But things will be different now. I promise you. They will! *(Beat.)* Philip Adrian… such strong, beautiful hands! I want you to come home! We need you back in our lives! You hurt us so much with that lie, but we forgive you. We forgive you… because we love you. *(Beat.)* It *was*… just a lie… wasn't it? *(Silence.)* Answer me. *(Beat.)* Speak.

*(**Adrian** begins to laugh.)*

What are you laughing at? *(Pause.)* What are you laughing at? Philip? Philip? What is he laughing at? *(Beat.)* Stop it! *(Pause.)* Stop it! Philip? Philip? Tell him to stop it! *(Beat.)* Is it true? *(Beat.)* Is it true? Answer me! *(Beat.)* Speak!

*(**Adrian** continues to laugh.)*

Is it true? Is it true? Oh, God… please God… no…

*(She runs to **Philip**, clutches him.)*

Philip? Tell me it's not true! Philip? *Tell me it's not true!* This is not how it's supposed to be! This is not how it's supposed to be! *(Beat.)* So you *do* want to destroy us! You *do* want to bring us down! Well it won't work. You know why? Because you're dead. *You're dead!* Glory be to God in heaven you're dead! *You're dead!* There's nothing I hate more than having a pervert's corpse in my house! So get out of my house! *Get out!!!*

(She draws her hand back, almost slaps him but doesn't. **Adrian** *stops laughing. Silence.)*

I'm sorry. *(Pause.)* I'm sorry. I couldn't help it. You hurt me. *(Silence.)* You're not dead… you can never be dead… you're here… even when you're not here. *(Pause.)* When I look at you now, when I look at what you've… become… it makes me wonder why I ever tried, why I ever bothered… pretending. *(Beat.)* When I look at you now, when I look at what you've… become… this table, this vase of azaleas, these chairs, these walls… amount to nothing. Absolutely nothing. The filth sweeps in… through the cracks in these walls… the grudges, the lies, the secrets… the things you say in the heat of anger which you say you don't mean but do, the silences between the words, the things you hide your eyes behind, the hands you caress but which refuse to caress back… and the little things: the socks you forget to clean, the tiles in the bathroom you forget to scrub, the earrings you drop in some dingy motel room while your husband's best friend is busy swallowing your neck.

(Silence.)

And you… *you…* so self-righteous and smug, mocking us, laughing at us, thinking you're so much better than us, untouched by the filth because you managed to get out. *(**Mary** stands, crosses to **Adrian**, stage right.)* Well, I've got news for you: you didn't get out! You'll never get out! The reason you're what you are is because of us. *Us!* And you'll wear that scar for the rest of your life. *(Beat.)* Just because you got out… or *think* you got out... doesn't mean the rest of us want to. *(MARY crosses to stage left.)* Did it ever occur to you that there are other things beyond one's own self-centred existence? Can't you show a little—respect—for those of us who've persevered, who've carried on with what's right... and what's normal? *(Beat.)* Your father wants you dead. He wants to *think* that you're dead. I never understood why, but I think I do now. *(Beat.)* When we see this table, this vase of azaleas, these chairs, these walls, what we see... is death. Not the epic whittling away of the body... the way it often is for people like you... but another kind of death, one that's beautiful and right, that *click* that turns everything pure white. The world's crystal clear when you're dead. It makes you wonder why you were ever alive.

*(**MARY** crosses to behind **PHILIP**.)*

Your father is dead. And I suppose so am I. He wants to *think* that you're dead. If he doesn't then we're... *alive...* and this... simplicity... will end. *(Pause.)* Your father doesn't hate you... he *really* doesn't hate you. In some strange way I think he admires you. But he wants you *dead*, so that *we* can be dead. So go away... please... and let us die.

*(**ADRIAN** exits stage right. **MARY** returns to the chaise, sits, folds clothes.)*

MARY: Philip.

PHILIP: Mary. *(Silence.)* Happy anniversary. *(Pause.)* My darling.

*Tanja Dixon-Warren as **Mary** and Michael Fera as **Phillp** in "Hands."*
Photo by Mélissa C. Powell.

Scene 9

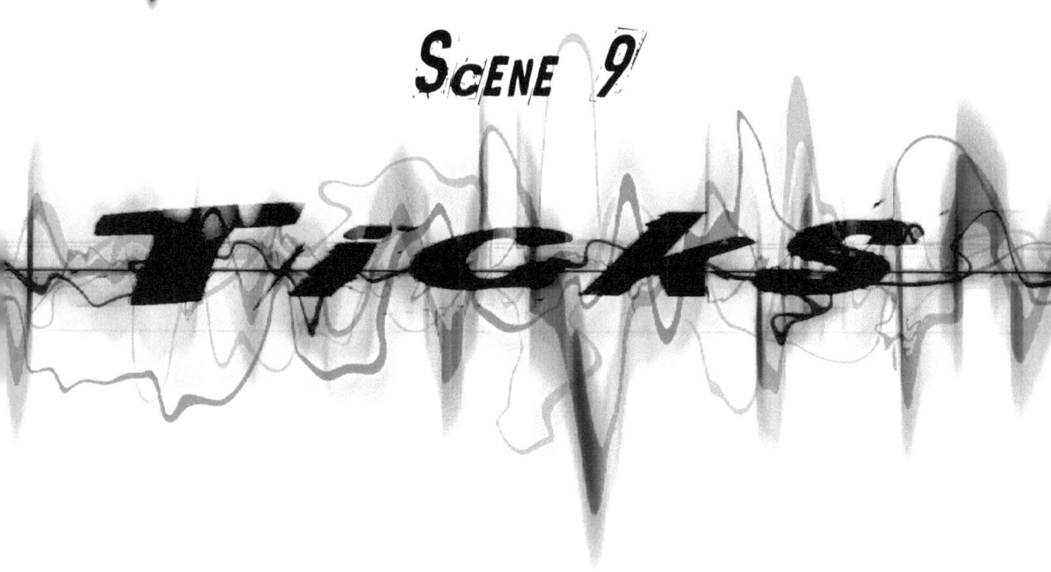

*(**Adrian** enters stage left.)*

Adrian: Light.

*(Light on **Adrian**. He is facing the audience. Both his voice and the city sounds crescendo as the speech progresses. The tempo is fast again.)*

You're my city, this is my show, you're my city, this is my show, do you know how I got this huge black hole, do you know how I got this huge black hole, well in the end, from you, *you*, 'cause I've watched you, all of you, every day, every night, you're working downtown and you're coughing, coughing, till everyone around you is coughing, coughing, and finally the day ends and you pile onto the street, and you start bumping into people and coughing in their face, and then they start coughing and the whole city starts coughing, and cars are crashing and buses are colliding 'cause the guys at the wheel are coughing, coughing, and people go home and their families start coughing, and soon all the suburbs 'round the city are coughing, and finally night comes and you're coughing into the club, where night after night there's jazz fast as light, and you're coughing in my face and I'm breathing it all in, and you're coughing in my face and I'm breathing it all in, and soon a black hole begins to form in my chest, it grows wider and wider and deeper and deeper, 'til finally it's as wide and deep as a dungeon, and the city breaks in, invades my hole, the dirt, the filth, the piss, the shit, the telephones ringing, the taxi cabs honking, the buses, the cars, the buildings, the malls, the brushes and the bumps, the forgotten I'm sorry's, the sideway glances, the cursory hellos, the unreturned calls, the meaningless chats, the tears that fall ever so lightly into your drink, and it's all pouring in, it's burning my hole, the talking and the laughing and the clinking and the fucking, and the jazz from the club all night every night, jazz from the club all night fast as light, the city has polluted my body, my soul, but fuck it's me who's gonna die not you, *(Crying.)* the city has polluted my body, my soul, but fuck it's me who's gonna die, not you, *(Almost lunging into the audience.)* ARE YOU DEAF OR IS THE JAZZ STILL RINGING IN YOUR EAR, SITTING THERE LIKE YOU HAVEN'T GOT A CLUE IN THE WORLD, ARE YOU DEAF OR IS THE JAZZ STILL RINGING IN YOUR EAR, SITTING THERE LIKE YOU HAVEN'T GOT A CLUE IN THE WORLD, *(Evangelical.)* THIS COULD'VE BEEN YOU BUT IT'S ME, IT'S ME, I'M DYING FOR YOU AND FOR THE HOLE IN YOUR SOUL, SO GET DOWN ON YOUR KNEES AND PRAY FOR FORGIVENESS, MY SICK, POLLUTED LITTLE CITY!

(The city sounds reach fff.)

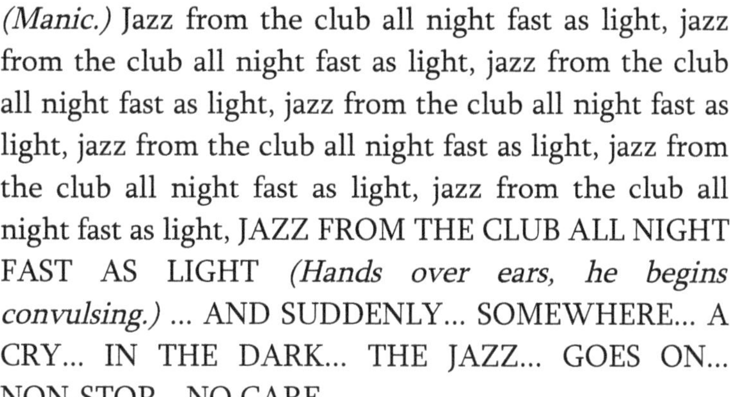

(Manic.) Jazz from the club all night fast as light, jazz from the club all night fast as light, jazz from the club all night fast as light, jazz from the club all night fast as light, jazz from the club all night fast as light, jazz from the club all night fast as light, jazz from the club all night fast as light, JAZZ FROM THE CLUB ALL NIGHT FAST AS LIGHT *(Hands over ears, he begins convulsing.)* ... AND SUDDENLY... SOMEWHERE... A CRY... IN THE DARK... THE JAZZ... GOES ON... NON-STOP... NO CARE...

(The city sounds are still fff.)

Down.
Down.
DOWN!

(The city sounds fade out.)

But the hole is the truth. The hole is the Word.
Tick.
Tick.
TICK!

(Somewhere, a metronome begins to tick. It ticks seven times before ADRIAN *resumes speaking. As at the beginning of the play, each line end and accent symbol in the following speech coincides with another tick of the metronome.)*

(Imperiously.) Í! *(Tick.)*
Am your háilstorm! *(Tick.)*
Your eárthquake! *(Tick.)*
Your líght! *(Tick.)*

The bówl. *(Tick.)*
I hóld. *(Tick.)*
In my hánds. *(Tick.)*
The ánswer. *(Tick.)*
Is míne. *(Tick.)*

*(**Adrian** takes off his shirt. There are lesions on his torso.)*

Níght. *(Tick.)*
After níght. *(Tick.)*
Jázz. *(Tick.)*
Fast as líght. *(Tick.)*
Wínk. Nód. Jóin. *(Tick.)*
Súddenly. *(Tick.)*
Wíngs. *(Tick.)*
Flíght. *(Tick.)*
To the sún. *(Tick.)*
Flíght. *(Tick.)*
From níght. *(Tick.)*
Your crý. *(Tick.)*
A pléa. *(Tick.)*
For lóve. *(Tick.)*
For líght. *(Tick.)*
Sixty-fóur. *(Tick.)*
Sixty fíve. *(Tick.)*
Sixty-síx. *(Tick.)*
Sixty-séven. *(Tick.)*
Sixty-éight. *(Tick.)*
Sixty-níne. *(Tick.)*
Séventy. *(Tick.)*
Sixty-fóur. *(Tick.)*
Fémale. *(Tick.)*

*(**Woman 4** appears behind right scrim.)*

Mídnight. *(Tick.)*
Párk. *(Tick.)*
Wínk. Nód. Jóin. *(Tick.)*
Sixty-fíve. *(Tick.)*
Mále. *(Tick.)*

*(**Man 5** appears behind left scrim.)*

Mídnight. *(Tick.)*
Bár. *(Tick.)*
Wínk. Nód. Jóin. *(Tick.)*
Sixty-síx. *(Tick.)*
Fémale. *(Tick.)*

*(**Woman 5** appears behind right scrim.)*

Mídnight. *(Tick.)*
Bánk. *(Tick.)*
Wínk. Nód. Jóin. *(Tick.)*
Sixty-séven. *(Tick.)*
Mále. *(Tick.)*

*(**Man 6** appears behind left scrim.)*

Mídnight. *(Tick.)*
Stóre. *(Tick.)*
Wínk. Nód. Jóin. *(Tick.)*
Sixty-éight. *(Tick.)*
Fémale. *(Tick.)*
Mídnight. *(Tick.)*
Púmp. *(Tick.)*
Wínk. Nód. Jóin. *(Tick.)*
Sixty-níne. *(Tick.)*
Mále. *(Tick.)*

Mídnight. *(Tick.)*
Cáfe. *(Tick.)*
Wínk. Nód. Jóin. *(Tick.)*
Séventy. *(Tick.)*
Just a chíld. *(Tick.)*
Mídnight. *(Tick.)*
Chúrch. *(Tick.)*
Wínk. Nód. Jóin. *(Tick.)*
Chíld. *(Tick.)*
In whíte. *(Tick.)*
The cíty. *(Tick.)*
Will kíll. *(Tick.)*
Chíld. *(Tick.)*
In whíte. *(Tick.)*
I sáved. *(Tick.)*
From the dárk. *(Tick.)*
Níght. *(Tick.)*

(City sounds begin to crescendo.)

After níght. *(Tick.)*
After níght. *(Tick.)*
After níght. *(Tick.)*
After níght. *(Tick.)*
After níght. *(Tick.)*
After—

(Lights out.)

THE END

Tanja Dixon-Warren as **Mary** *and Thrasso Petras as* **Adrian** *in "Hands."*

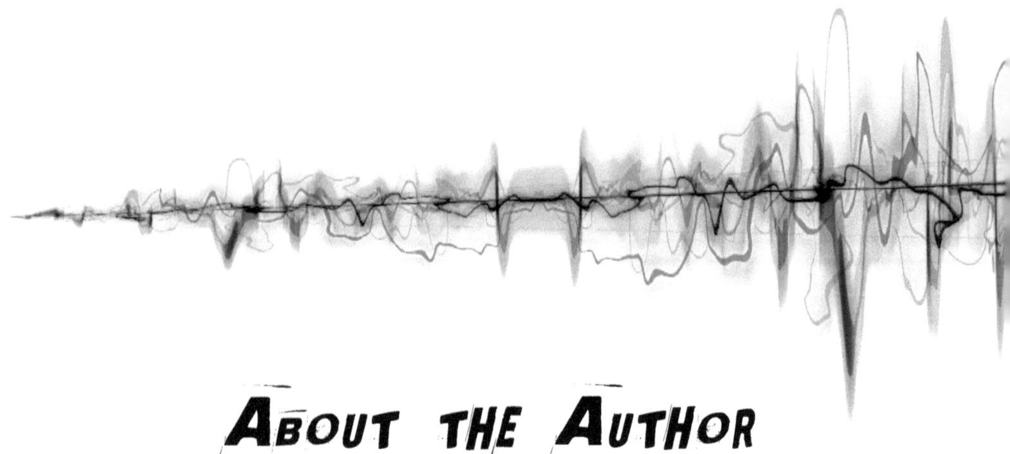

About the Author

C.E. Gatchalian was born in Vancouver in 1974. He is an alumnus of the University of British Columbia's Creative Writing program (BFA, 1996; MFA, 2002). His work has appeared on stages in both Vancouver and Toronto, as well as on television (the Bravo! Channel, the Knowledge Network) and radio (CBC Radio). His published collection of one-act plays, *Motifs & Repetitions & Other Plays*, was a finalist for the 2003 Lambda Literary Award, which honours the best in lesbian, gay, bisexual and transgendered literature in English. In 2005 he was awarded the Gordon Armstrong Playwright's Rent Award, which is awarded annually to a British Columbian playwright of merit. He is also a published fictionist and poet (his chapbook of poetry, *tor/sion*, was published the same year by Ottawa's Ransom Works Press). Currently Playwright-in-Residence at the Firehall Arts Centre, he was Writer-in-Residence at the Berton House Writers' Retreat in Dawson City, YT from July to September 2006. Visit his website at www.cegatchalian.com to learn more.

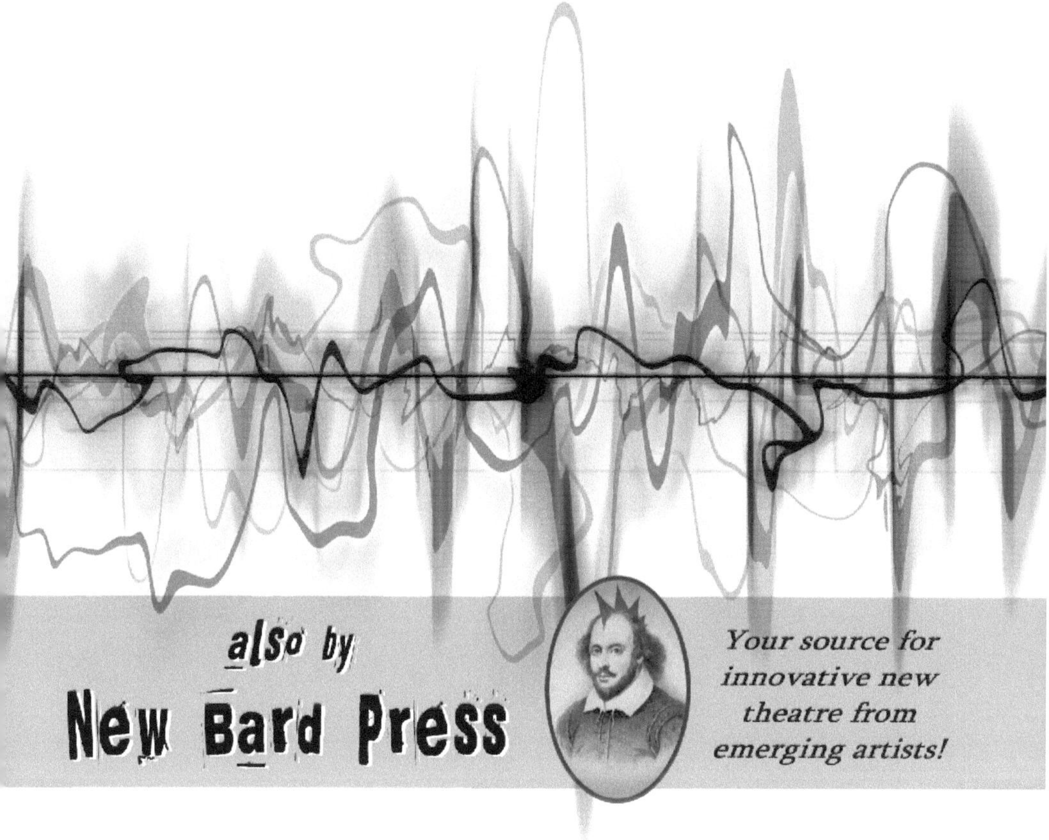

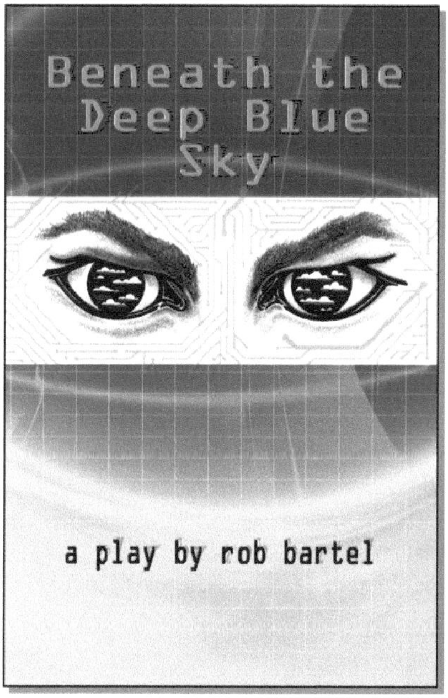

Ask your local bookseller for a copy of *Beneath the Deep Blue Sky,* a strange and stirring geek fantasia written for the stage by award winning poet, playwright, and computer game designer, Rob Bartel.

Schizophrenic internet addicts, dispossessed panhandlers, Soviet game programmers, digital Mozarts, defeated chess grandmasters, voyeuristic search engines and more chase their varying destinies in this whirlwind exploration of what it means to be human in the age of the computer. The result is a daringly original piece of theatre that sparks the imagination and imprints itself upon the memory for years to come.

ISBN: *1-4116-1519-0* ***MSRP:*** *$11.95 USD*

www.ingramcontent.com/pod-product-compliance
Ingram Content Group UK Ltd.
Pitfield, Milton Keynes, MK11 3LW, UK
UKHW041929190726
13854UKWH00004B/1528